Valerie Thomas and Korky Paul

Winnie's Magic Wand

OXFORD
UNIVERSITY PRESS

Winnie the Witch jumped out of bed.
It was a special day. It was the day of the
Witches' Magic Show, and Winnie was
making a wonderful new spell.

She felt nervous.
'I hope nothing goes wrong,' she said.
Wilbur felt nervous too. I expect something
will go wrong, he thought.

This book belongs to

. . . .

7

Winnie's Magic Wand is based on an idea emailed to Korky Paul
by Mr John Fidler's Class Y2F, Akrotiri Primary School, Cyprus.

Endpapers by Ashley Richardson aged 10.
Thank you to Marcham Primary School for helping with the endpapers – K.P.

For Ron Heapy – V.T.
To Alexi – K.P.

OXFORD
UNIVERSITY PRESS

Great Clarendon Street, Oxford OX2 6DP

Oxford University Press is a department of the University of Oxford.
It furthers the University's objective of excellence in research, scholarship,
and education by publishing worldwide in

Oxford New York

Auckland Cape Town Dar es Salaam Hong Kong Karachi
Kuala Lumpur Madrid Melbourne Mexico City Nairobi
New Delhi Shanghai Taipei Toronto

With offices in

Argentina Austria Brazil Chile Czech Republic France Greece
Guatemala Hungary Italy Japan Poland Portugal Singapore
South Korea Switzerland Thailand Turkey Ukraine Vietnam

Oxford is a registered trade mark of Oxford University Press
in the UK and in certain other countries

First published 2002
Reprinted 2002
First published in paperback 2002
Reissued with new cover 2006
10 9

British Library Cataloguing in Publication Data
Data available

ISBN : 978-0-19-272644-5 (paperback)
ISBN : 978-0-19-272668-1 (paperback with audio CD)

Printed in Singapore

Paper used in the production of this book is a natural,
recyclable product made from wood grown in sustainable forests.
The manufacturing process conforms to the environmental
regulations of the country of origin.

www.korkypaul.com

'What shall I wear?' said Winnie.
She got out her party dress.
Oh no! She had spilt red jelly on it!

Winnie threw the dress into the washing machine.
Then she threw in her towels, her pyjamas,
and her stripy tights.

She turned on the washing machine.
Swish, swish, clunk, it went.

When the washing machine had finished
going swish, swish, clunk, Winnie took out
the clothes and hung them on the line.

But her magic wand had been
washed as well. Oh no!

'I hope it still works,'
Winnie said.

Winnie dried the wand with a towel.

'I'll try it out,' she said. 'Something
easy. I'll change this apple into
an orange.'

She closed her eyes, waved her wand, and shouted,

ABRACADABRA!

Suddenly there was an apple tree growing in her kitchen.
'Bother!' said Winnie. 'That wand's not working properly.'

Winnie dried the wand with her hair-drier.

'That's better,' she said. 'I'll try again.
I'll turn this apple tree back into an apple again.'
She picked up the wand, and shouted,

ABRACADABRA!

This time, the apple tree turned into an enormous apple pie.

'Oh no! *Oh no!*' Winnie moaned.
Now she really was worried.
It was nearly time for the Magic Show.
The wonderful new spell would be a disaster.

Wilbur was worried too.

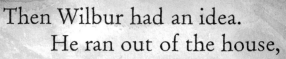

Then Wilbur had an idea.
He ran out of the house,

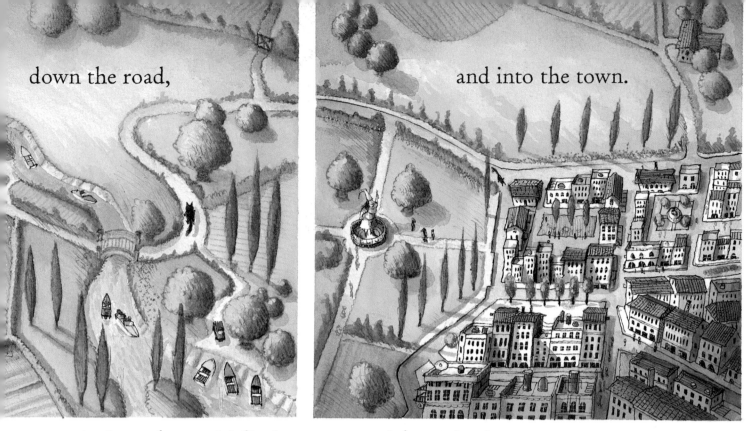

down the road,

and into the town.

Perhaps *he* could find a new wand for Winnie.
He looked in all the shops.

But no magic wands.

Then, around the corner, he saw a little shop.
In the window was a big box of wands!

Wilbur grabbed one and galloped off home.

It was getting late.
Soon it would be too late for the Magic
Show. Winnie was very, very worried.

What could she do?

Then Wilbur ran through the cat flap with the new wand.

'Oh Wilbur!' cried Winnie. 'You are a clever cat.'

She didn't even have time to put on her party dress.
She jumped on her broomstick,
Wilbur jumped onto her shoulder,
and off they went.

They arrived just in time for Winnie's spell.
Everyone was sitting there, feeling excited.
Winnie always did something special.

'First,' announced Winnie, 'I will turn my
beautiful black cat into a green cat.'

She waved her wand, and shouted,

ABRACADABRA!

Wilbur waited . . .
       Everyone waited . . .

Winnie tried again.

Nothing.

At last, a bunch of paper flowers
popped out of the end of
the trick wand.

One of the witches started to laugh.
Soon everyone was laughing.
They laughed, they screamed,
they shrieked and fell off their chairs.

'What a clever joke, Winnie,' they cried.
'Where did you get that wand?'
Winnie smiled. But she didn't say anything.

And neither did Wilbur.

SPOT THE DIFFERENCES

CROW OR RAVEN?

Bullfrog Books